Once upon  was a scien... She loved to ... robots.

THIS SIDE UP ↑

AGILE
DLE WITH CARE

Out of This World Inc.

Sue

TRUST ME I'M A GENIUS

MAD SCIENTIST

There was one teeny problem. Sue couldn't figure out which part was which or what part went where.

Sue made mixed-up robots and called them FRANKENBOTS!

FRANKENSTEIN WAS SUE'S FAVORITE MOVIE MONSTER OF ALL TIME.

Frankenbots came in all shapes and sizes with rivets, spikes, and bolts.

Some were powered by boilers, others by solar volts.

There were bots as small as a flea and bots as tall as a tree.

Lots and lots of bots.
Singers, dancers, mechanics...
even astronauts.

Stu helped Sue make lunch,

OOPS!

CRASH!

clean her room,

and do her homework, especially the science project parts.

my science project
the Bog
Franken Dog!

Every morning,
Sue waved goodbye to Stu.
And, every day,
Stu followed Sue to school.

He wanted to go to school, too.

They launched Stu and
the Frankenbots into space.

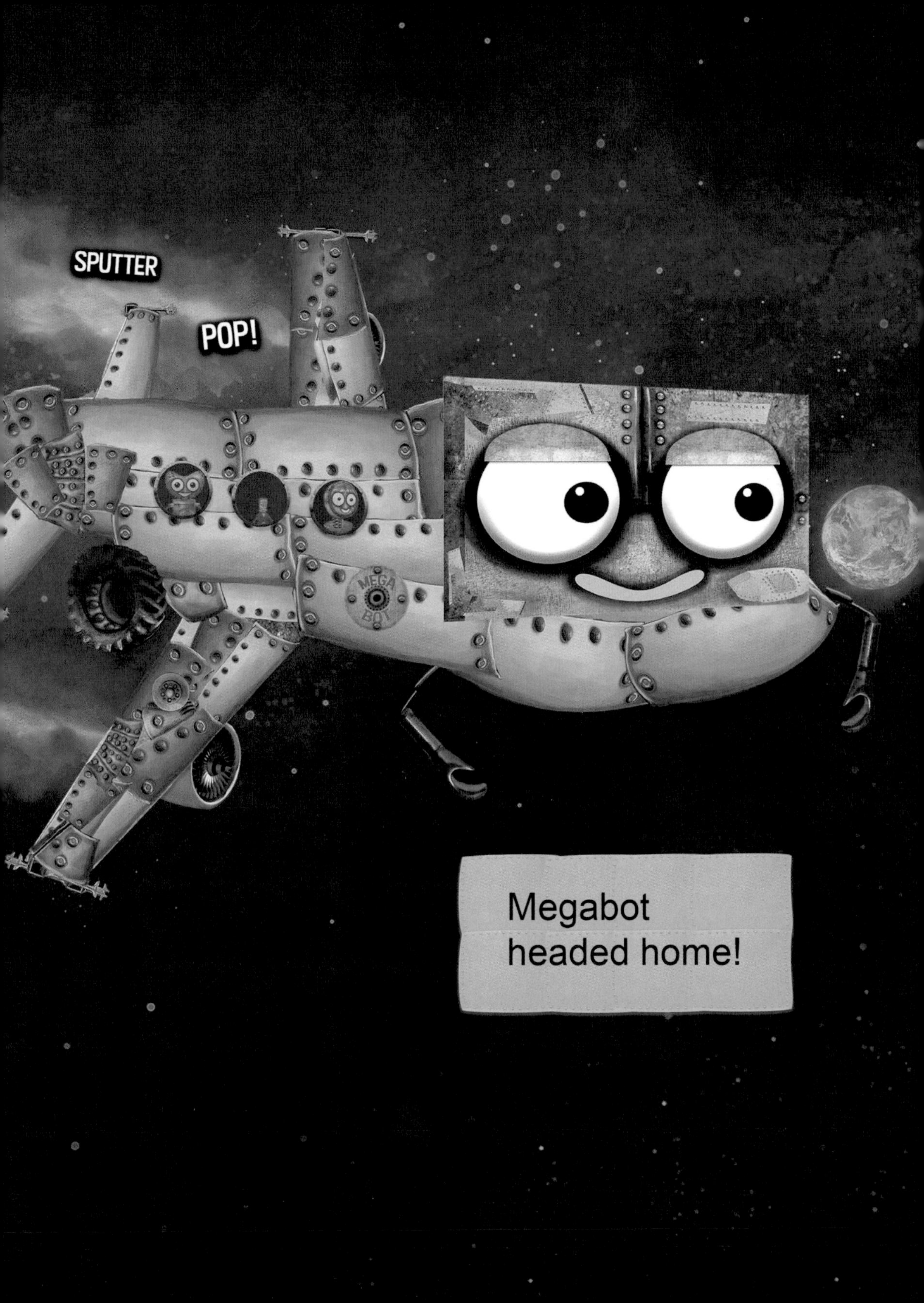


Megabot
headed home!

MEGABOT landed with mega JOLTS,
and all the Shadowbots lost their bolts.

People cheered for the bots who were brave.

How many Frankenbots can you spot?

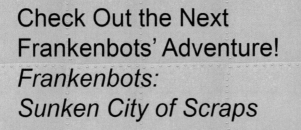

Check Out the Next
Frankenbots' Adventure!
*Frankenbots:*
*Sunken City of Scraps*

Did you know there is a little
Frankenstein on every page of
this book?
Did you find them all?

Made in the USA
Middletown, DE
27 February 2021